The *St Michael* ® book of

Winnie the Pooh

Favourites

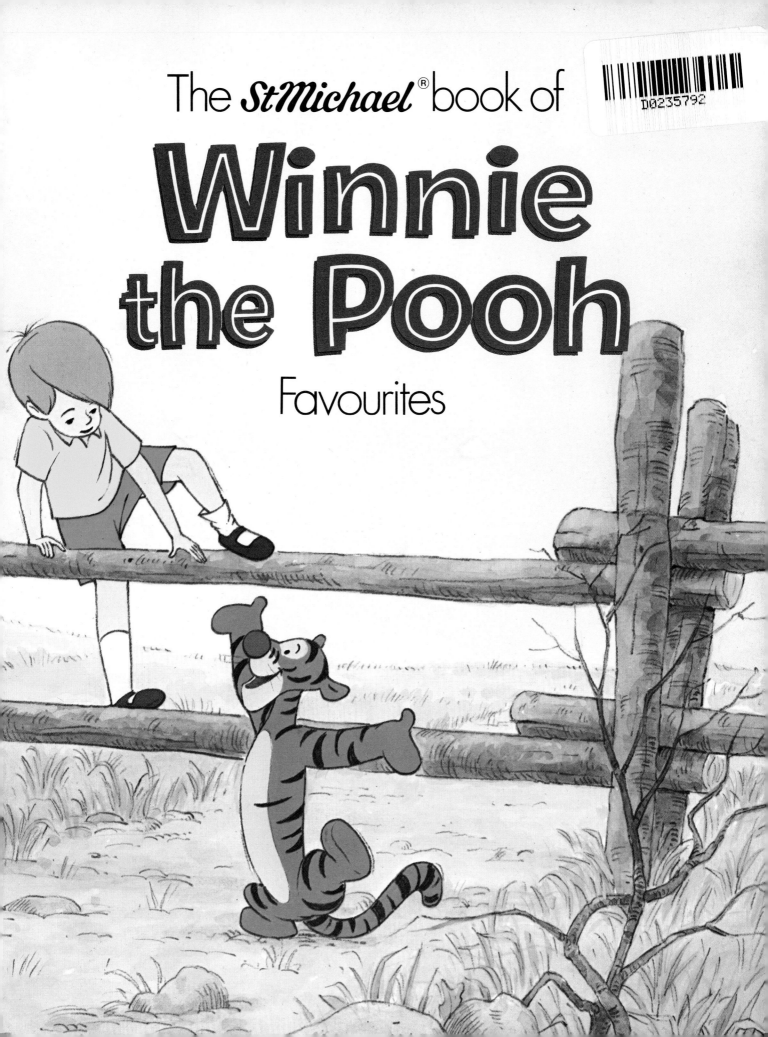

Winnie the Pooh
and the
Blustery Day

ONE blustery day Winnie the Pooh decided to visit his thoughtful spot and on the way he made up a little hum, and it hummed something like this: "Hum dum dum di di dum, hum, dum, dum. Oh the wind is lashing lustily, and the trees are thrashing thrustily, and the leaves are rustling gustily, so it's rather safe to say, that it seems . . . that it may turn out to be . . . it feels that it will undoubtedly . . . it looks like a rather blustery day today. It seems that it may turn out to be, feels that it will . . . undoubtedly . . . looks like a rather blustery day today."

Fortunately, Pooh's thoughtful spot was in a sheltered place and now he sat down and tried hard to think of something. While Pooh Bear was thinking, a gopher popped up out of his hole.

"If I were you, I'd think about skedaddlin' out of here," said the gopher to Pooh.

"Why?" asked Pooh.

"Because it's Windsday," said the gopher and popped back into his hole.

Pooh thought for a moment and then said to himself,
"Windsday? Oh, ah . . . oh. Then I think I shall wish everyone
a Happy Windsday, and I shall begin with my very dear
friend, Piglet."

Now, Piglet lived in the middle of the forest, in a very grand
house, in the middle of a beech tree, and Piglet loved it. . . .

Outside Piglet's house was a sign which once had said
'TRESPASSERS WILL BE PROSECUTED', but now, because
it had broken in half, only said 'TRESPASSERS WILL'.

According to Piglet the house had belonged to his grandfather, and Piglet said his grandfather's name was Trespassers Will. This was short, said Piglet, for Trespassers William and his grandma had called him T.W., which was even shorter. Well, on this blustery day, the wind was giving Piglet a bit of a bother. Piglet said to himself, "I don't mind the leaves that are leaving, it's the leaves that are coming."

Just as he finished speaking he was swept up and blown along on a large leaf. As Piglet was being blown along he flew past Pooh Bear who was on his way to wish Piglet a Happy Windsday.

"Where are you going, Piglet?" asked Pooh.

"That's what I'm asking myself. Where? Whew . . . whoops," said Piglet.

Pooh grabbed hold of Piglet's scarf as he flew by.

"Oh, Pooh," cried Piglet.

"And what do you think you will answer yourself?" asked Pooh, rather worried.

"Oh, Pooh, I'm unravelling," said Piglet.

And he was. His scarf unravelled and he went high into the air, as high as a kite, while Pooh was left on the ground holding the other end of the unravelling scarf.

The scarf went on unravelling until there was no scarf left, only a string of wool. Piglet quickly grabbed hold of the end of the string.

"Oh . . . that . . . that was a c . . . c . . . close one," said Piglet, softly.

"Hang on tight, Piglet," called Pooh, who was running along the ground holding on to the other end of the string.

Piglet flew over fields and hedges and all the time Pooh was running along beneath him. They came, after a while, to Kanga's house, and Roo, who was in his mother's pouch, called, "Look, Mama, look, a kite!"

"Oh, my goodness," said Kanga, "it's Piglet!"

"Happy Windsday, Kanga. Happy Windsday, Roo," said Pooh, as he rushed by.

"Can I fly Piglet next, Pooh?" asked Roo.

But Pooh didn't hear him; he was going too fast.

Eeyore had spent most of the morning building a lean-to of sticks.

"That should stand up against anything," he said, as he put the last stick on the pile. But it didn't, because at that very moment, along swept Pooh Bear and he went right through Eeyore's lean-to and left just a pile of sticks.

"Happy Windsday, Eeyore," said Pooh.

"Thanks for noticing me," said Eeyore.

On and on swept Pooh and Piglet. Pooh was being bounced along the ground.

Rabbit was picking carrots from his carrot patch when along came Pooh digging his feet into the ground.

"Happy Windsday, Rabbit," called Pooh.

"Pooh Bear, stop! Oh, go back. Oh, no!" cried Rabbit. He picked up his wheelbarrow and ran after Pooh.

Pooh's feet dug up all Rabbit's carrots and they flew up into the air and landed in Rabbit's wheelbarrow. Rabbit was very pleased and said to himself, "Next time, I hope he blows right through my rhubarb patch."

Suddenly, Pooh was lifted right off the ground and flew along with Piglet. The two of them were blown right up to the window of Owl's house.

"Who, who, who, who is it?" said Owl, who heard Piglet knocking on the window.

"It's me. P-p-p-please, may I come in?" called Piglet.

"Well, I say now, someone has pasted Piglet on my window," said Owl.

Then Pooh bumped into the window.

". . . Pooh, too. This is a surprise," laughed Owl. "Well, it's very nice to see you both," said Owl.

The house was being blown backwards and forwards, and Owl started to tell Pooh and Piglet about an even worse wind he remembered. Just then, the tree with Owl's house in fell down with a crash. Owl was asking Pooh if he had knocked the tree down, when along came Christopher Robin and Eeyore.

"What a pity, Owl, I don't think we will ever be able to mend it," said Christopher Robin.

"If you ask me, when a house looks like that, it's time to find another one," said Eeyore. "Might take a day or two, but I'll find a new one."

Later, the blustery day turned into a very blustery night. Pooh Bear was in his house and heard a very strange noise outside. The noise sounded like this: "Rrrrrrrr!"

"Oh . . . is that you, Piglet?" said Pooh, rather frightened.

"Rrrr," said the noise.

"Well, tell me about it tomorrow, Eeyore," said Pooh, as he jumped under the covers on his bed.

"Rrrrrr," said the noise again.

"Oh, come in, Christopher Robin," said Pooh.

Now Pooh, being a bear of very little brain, decided to invite the new sound in.

"Hello out there. Oh, I hope nobody answers," he said.

"Rrrrrr. Hello, I'm Tigger," said Tigger.

"Oh," said Pooh. "Oh . . . oh . . . you scared me."

Tigger had bounced right on top of Pooh and knocked him
on to the floor.

"Oh, I'm sure I did. Everyone's scared of Tiggers. And who
are you?" laughed Tigger.

"I'm Pooh," said Pooh.

"Oh, ah, Pooh. Ah . . . !" he said. "What's a Pooh?"

"You're sitting on one."

Tigger shook his head.

"I am? Oh, well, glad to meet you. Name's Tigger," and he climbed off Pooh. "T–I . . . double guh—er. That spells Tigger."

"But what is a Tigger?" asked Pooh.

"Well, ha, ha, ha, he asked for it. Ho, ho," said Tigger, and sang this song.

". . . The wonderful thing about Tiggers is Tiggers are wonderful things,

Their tops are made out of rubber, their bottoms are made out of springs,

They're bouncy, trouncy, flouncy, pouncy, fun, fun, fun, fun, fun,

But the most wonderful thing about Tiggers is I'm the only one.

I'm the only one. Rrrrrrr."

"Then what's that over there?" asked Pooh, pointing to the mirror.

"Huh? Oh, hey, hey, look, look what a strange-looking creature. Hmm. Look at those beady little eyes, and that pur-posti-rus chin, and those ricky-diculus striped pyjamas," said Tigger.

"Looks like another Tigger to me," said Pooh.

"Oh, no, it's not. I'm the only Tigger. Watch me scare the stripes off this impostor."

Tigger growled into the mirror and saw himself growling back. He was so frightened that he hid under the table.

"Is he gone?" asked Tigger.

"Yes," said Pooh. "You can come out now, Tigger."

"I'm hungry," said Tigger.

Pooh asked if he liked honey, hoping he would say no.

"Tiggers love honey," said Tigger.

"Oh dear," said Pooh, but gave Tigger a jar of honey.

Tigger dropped his paw into the honey and tasted it.

"Ugh, Tiggers don't like honey," he said.

"But you said that you liked . . ." said Pooh, but before he could finish Tigger said:

"Yes, that icky sticky stuff is only fit for Heffalumps and Woozles."

"You mean Elephants . . . and Weasels," said Pooh.

"That's what I said. Heffalumps and Woozles."

"Well, well, what do heff ah . . . ah . . . hallalaff, ah . . . what do they do?" asked Pooh.

"Oh, nothing much. Just steal honey."

"Steal honey?" cried Pooh, grabbing his honey pot.

"Yes, they do. Well, I'd better be bouncing along now . . ." said Tigger, and off he went singing his song.

Pooh said goodbye to Tigger and thought about Heffalumps and Woozles. He got his toy gun and decided to guard his honey. As he marched up and down, Pooh talked to himself in the mirror.

"Oh, hello. Am I glad to see you. It's more friendly with two. Now, you go that way and I'll go this way. You didn't see anything, did you? Neither did I."

Pooh marched for hour after hour after hour, guarding his honey. The blustery day had now turned into a very rainy night. Pooh kept marching, until at last he fell fast asleep and

began to dream. He dreamt about Heffalumps and Woozles and this is the song they sang:

"Heffalumps and Woozles. Heffalumps and Woozles . . . steal honey. Beware. Beware. They're black, they're brown, they're up, they're down. They're in, they're out, they're all about. They're far, they're near, they're gone, they're here. They're quick and slick, they're insincere. Beware. Beware. Beware. Beware. Beware. A Heffalump or Woozle is very confusil. A Heffalump or Woozle's very sly, sly, sly, sly, they come in ones and twosles, but if they so choozles, before your eyes you'll see them multiply, ply, ply, ply. They're extraordinary, so better be wary, because they come in every shape and size, size, size, size. If honey's what you covet, you'll find that they love it, because they'll guzzle up the thing you prize. They're green, they're blue, they're pink, they're white. They're round, they're square, they're a terrible sight, they tie themselves in horrible knots, they come in stripes or polka dots. Beware, beware, be a very wary bear."

Outside Pooh's house it rained and rained and rained all through the night. When Pooh woke up in the morning his house was flooded with water, so he gathered up his honey pots and climbed the highest tree he could find.

Meanwhile Piglet's house had flooded too and Piglet had just written a note and put it in a bottle. The note said 'HELP, PIGLET' and Piglet had just put it in the bottle when he was washed right out of his house on a chair and along past Pooh, who was sitting in the tree. Just then Pooh was knocked off his tree and landed in a honey pot. So Pooh in his honey pot and Piglet in his chair were swept along in the flood.

And the Hundred Acre Wood got floodier and floodier. But the water couldn't come up to Christopher Robin's house . . . so that's where everyone was gathering. It was a time of great excitement. But in the middle of the excitement Eeyore stuck stubbornly to his task of house-hunting for Owl.

Meanwhile, on Christopher Robin's island, Little Roo made an important discovery. He had found Piglet's note. Christopher Robin read the note and told everyone that Piglet was lost and they would have to rescue him. Owl flew off to search for Piglet and after a while he spotted Pooh and Piglet being swept along in the flood. He flew down and guided Pooh and Piglet back to Christopher Robin's island.

When they got to the island Pooh was sitting on the chair and Piglet had been swept into the honey pot.

"Hallo, Pooh," said Christopher Robin. "Thank goodness you're safe. Have you seen Piglet?"

At that moment Piglet popped out of the honey pot.

"Excuse me, I have . . . Oh, what I mean is . . . here I am," said Piglet.

"Pooh, you rescued Piglet," said Christopher Robin.

"I did?" said Pooh.

"Yes," said Christopher Robin. "You are very brave, and as soon as this flood is over I shall give you a hero party."

The next day the flood was over and everybody except Eeyore was at Christopher Robin's hero party for Pooh. Christopher Robin was saying, "Attention everybody, this is a hero party for Pooh," when along came Eeyore.

"I found it," he said.

"Found what, Eeyore?" asked Christopher Robin.

"A house for Owl," said Eeyore. "Follow me."

They all followed Eeyore and he took them to Piglet's house.

"Why are you stopping here, Eeyore?" asked Christopher Robin.

"This is it," said Eeyore.

"Oh, dear," said Piglet.

"Name's on it," said Eeyore. "W – O – L spells Owl."

"Bless my soul, so it does," said Owl.

"Well, what do you think of it?" asked Eeyore.

"It is a nice house, Eeyore, but . . ." said Christopher Robin.

"It is a lovely house, Eeyore . . ." said Kanga, "but, but . . ."

"It's the best house in the whole world," Piglet sobbed.

"Tell them it's your house, Piglet," said Pooh.

"No, Pooh," said Piglet. "This house belongs to our very good friend, Owl."

"But, Piglet, where will you live?" asked Rabbit.

"Well, I . . . I-I-I guess I shall live ah . . . (sniff) I-I-I-suppose I-I-shall live . . ." sniffed Piglet.

"With me. You shall live with me, won't you, Piglet?" cried Pooh.

"With you? Oh, thank you, Pooh Bear. Of course I will," said Piglet.

"Piglet, that was a very grand thing to do," said Christopher Robin.

"A heroic thing to do," said Rabbit.

"Christopher Robin, can you make a one-hero party into a two-hero party?" asked Pooh.

"Of course we can, silly old bear," said Christopher Robin.

So Pooh was a hero for saving Piglet, and Piglet was a hero for giving Owl his grand home in the beech tree, and the two heroes had a lovely party with all their friends.

And so the blustery day turned out to be not so bad after all.

Winnie the Pooh lived in a forest all by himself, under the name of Sanders. This name was written in gold letters over the door of his house, and looked very grand.

One day when Pooh was out walking, he came to a wide open space in the middle of the forest and in the middle of the space was a large oak-tree and from the top of the tree Pooh could hear a loud buzzing noise.

Winnie the Pooh sat down at the foot of the tree, put his head between his paws and began to think. He thought very slowly. First of all he said to himself, "That buzzing noise means something. You don't get a buzzing noise unless someone is making a buzzing noise and the only thing that I know that makes a buzzing noise is a bee. And the only thing that bees do is make honey!"

He got up and said, "And I *love* honey." So he began to climb the tree.

He
climbed
and
he
climbed
and
he
climbed
and
as
he
climbed
he
sang
a
song
to
himself
because
he
liked
to
sing.

Then he climbed a little further . . . and a little further . . . and a little further. He was nearly there, and if he could just stand on one branch higher he could reach the honey. Then there was a sudden loud crack, and before he could say 'Christopher Robin', he fell head over heels to the bottom of the tree and landed in a gorse bush.

"Oh, help!" said Pooh.

He crawled out of the gorse bush, brushed the prickles from his nose and began to think about getting some help. And the first person he thought of was his friend, Christopher Robin.

So Winnie the Pooh went round to see him. Christopher Robin lived behind a green door in another part of the forest.

He was very pleased to see his little friend Pooh, but was rather puzzled when Pooh asked him if he had a balloon.

"A balloon?"

"Yes," said Pooh. "You see, I'm trying to reach some honey and I've got to have a balloon to get there."

"But you don't get honey with balloons," said Christopher Robin, laughing.

"I do," said Winnie the Pooh seriously.

"Well, I just happen to have two," said Christopher Robin. "Which would you like, blue or green?"

Pooh put his head between his paws and thought carefully.

"When you go after honey with a balloon," he said, "the great thing is not to let the bees see you. So I think I'll try the blue balloon and maybe the bees will think I'm part of the sky. Oh dear, but they might notice me underneath. I'll pretend to be a little black cloud."

So off they went, and Winnie the Pooh rolled in some mud until he was black all over. Then he took hold of the balloon by its string and up and away he went, right to the very top of the tree. The only trouble was, he was twenty feet away from the honey.

"This is wonderful," shouted Winnie the Pooh. "I feel just like a little black cloud!"

"You don't look very much like a cloud," called Christopher Robin.

"Oh, well, maybe the bees won't notice," replied Pooh.

And there he stayed. But there was no wind to blow him nearer the tree and after a while he began to get just the tiniest bit worried. He could see the honey; he could smell the honey, but he couldn't get any nearer to it. The bees were buzzing loudly in their nest and this worried Pooh even more.

"I think they suspect something," he called to Christopher Robin in a loud whisper. "Could you go and get your umbrella?"

"Well, I should think so," said Christopher Robin. "Will it help?"

"Yes, if you walk up and down with it and look up at me and say, 'Tut-tut, it looks like rain.' Then the bees would *know* I was a little black cloud."

So Christopher Robin went home and fetched his umbrella.

Pooh was quite anxious by the time he returned because the bees were now definitely suspicious and some of them had left their nest and were buzzing round Winnie the Pooh in an enquiring way.

The umbrella didn't seem to make any difference and all of a sudden Pooh called down to Christopher Robin:

"Christopher Robin," called out the cloud.

"Yes?"

"I have just been thinking," said the cloud in a panicky sort of voice, "and I have come to a very important decision. *These are the wrong sort of bees.*"

"Are they?" said Christopher Robin.

"Quite the wrong sort," replied Pooh firmly. "So they'll make the wrong sort of honey, won't they?"

"I suppose they will."

"So I think I shall come down," went on Pooh.

"But how are you going to do that?" asked Christopher Robin.

But Winnie the Pooh hadn't thought about that at all. If he let go of the string he was sure to fall, and he didn't like that idea at all. So he thought for a very long time, then he said:

"You'll have to shoot the balloon with your gun, Christopher Robin."

Christopher Robin didn't think that was a very good idea.

"It will spoil the balloon, you know," he said.

"Yes, but if you don't, I shall have to let go and that will spoil *me*," said Pooh.

Christopher Robin could see what Pooh meant and so he aimed very carefully at the balloon and fired.

"Ouch!" said Pooh.

"Did I miss?" asked Christopher Robin.

"You didn't exactly *miss*," said Pooh ruefully, "but you missed the balloon."

"I'm sorry," said Christopher Robin, and fired again. This time he hit the balloon, the air came slowly out and Winnie the Pooh floated gently to the ground.

The trouble was that his arms were so stiff from holding on to the balloon for such a long time, that they stayed sticking up in the air for the rest of the week, and what is more, he never *did* get any of that lovely honey.

Winnie the Pooh
and Tigger Too

Now Kanga had felt rather motherly that morning, and Wanting to Count Things, like Roo's vests, and how many pieces of soap there were left, so she had sent Roo and Tigger out with some sandwiches to have a nice long morning in the Forest not getting into mischief.

And as they walked along, Tigger told Roo (who wanted to know) all about the things that Tiggers could do.

"Can they fly?" asked Roo.

"Yes," said Tigger, "they're very good flyers."

"Ooh!" said Roo. "Can they fly as well as Owl?"

"Yes," said Tigger. "Only they don't want to."

"Why don't they want to?"

"Well, they just don't like it, somehow."

Roo couldn't understand this, because he thought it would be lovely to be able to fly, but Tigger said it was difficult to explain.

"Well," said Roo, "can they jump as far as Kangas?"

"Yes," said Tigger. "When they want to."

"I *love* jumping," said Roo. "Let's see who can jump farthest, you or me."

"*I* can," said Tigger. "But we mustn't stop now, or we shall be late."

"Late for what?"

"For whatever we want to be in time for," said Tigger, hurrying on.

In a little while they came to the Six Pine Trees.

"I can swim," said Roo. "I fell into a river, and I swam. Can Tiggers swim?"

"Of course they can. Tiggers can do everything."

"Can they climb trees better than Pooh?" asked Roo, stopping under the tallest pine tree, and looking up at it.

"Climbing trees is what they do best," said Tigger. "Much better than Poohs."

"Could they climb this one?"

"They're always climbing trees like that," said Tigger. "Up and down all day."

"Ooh, Tigger, are they *really*?"

"I'll show you," said Tigger bravely, "and you can sit on my back and watch me." For of all the things he had said Tiggers could do, the only one he felt certain about was climbing trees. So Roo sat on Tigger's back and up they went.

And for the first ten feet Tigger said happily to himself, "Up we go!" And for the next ten feet he said: "I always *said* Tiggers could climb trees." And for the next ten feet he said: "Not that it's easy, mind you." And for the next ten feet he said: "Of course, there's the coming down too. Backwards." And then he said: "Which will be difficult . . . unless one fell . . . when it would be . . . EASY."

And at the word 'easy' the branch he was standing on broke suddenly, and he just managed to clutch at the one above him as he felt himself going . . . and then slowly he got his chin over it . . . and then one back paw . . . and then the other . . . until at last he was sitting on it, breathing very quickly, and wishing that he had gone in for swimming instead.

Roo climbed off, and sat down next to him.

"Ooh, Tigger," he said excitedly, "are we at the top?"

"No," said Tigger.

"Oh," said Roo rather sadly. And then he went on hopefully, "That was a lovely bit just now, when you pretended we were going to fall. Will you do that bit again?"

"NO," said Tigger.

Roo was silent for a little while, and then he said, "Shall we eat our sandwiches, Tigger?" And Tigger said, "Yes, where are they?" And Roo said, "At the bottom of the tree." And Tigger said, "I don't think we'd better eat them just yet." So they didn't.

By and by Pooh and Piglet came along.

"Look, Pooh!" said Piglet suddenly. "There's something in one of the pine trees."

"So there is!" said Pooh, looking up wonderingly. "There's an Animal."

"Pooh!" cried Piglet. "I think it's Tigger and Roo!"

"So it is," said Pooh.

"Hallo, Roo!" called Piglet. "What are you doing?"

"We can't get down, we can't get down!" cried Roo. "Isn't it fun? Pooh, isn't it fun, Tigger and I are living in a tree, like Owl, and we're going to stay here for ever and ever. I can see Piglet's house. Piglet, I can see your house from here. Aren't we high? Is Owl's house as high up as this?"

"How did you get there, Roo?" asked Piglet.

"On Tigger's back! And Tiggers can't climb downwards, because their tails get in the way, only upwards, and Tigger forgot about that when we started, and he's only just remembered. So we've got to stay here for ever and ever—unless we go higher. What do you say, Tigger? Oh,

Tigger says if we go higher we shan't be able to see Piglet's house so well, so we're going to stop here."

"Piglet," said Pooh, when he heard all this, "what shall we do?" And he began to eat Tigger's sandwiches.

"Are they stuck?" asked Piglet.

Pooh nodded.

"Couldn't you climb up to them?"

"I might be able to, Piglet, and I might be able to bring Roo down on my back, but I couldn't bring Tigger down. So we must think of something else." And as he thought he began to eat Roo's sandwiches, too.

Whether he would have thought of anything before he had finished the last sandwich, I don't know, but he had just got to the last but one when there was a crackling in the bracken, and Christopher Robin and Eeyore came along.

"I shouldn't be surprised if it hailed tomorrow," Eeyore was saying. "Blizzards and whatnot. Being fine today doesn't mean anything. It has no sig—what's that word? Well, it has none of that. It's just a small piece of weather."

"There's Pooh!" said Christopher Robin, who didn't much mind *what* it did tomorrow, as long as he was out in it. "Hallo, Pooh!"

"It's Christopher Robin!" said Piglet. "*He'll* know what to do."

They hurried up to him.

"Oh, Christopher Robin," began Pooh.

"And Eeyore," said Eeyore.

"Tigger and Roo are right up the Six Pine Trees, and they can't get down, and——"

"And as I was saying," put in Piglet, "if only Christopher Robin——"

"*And* Eeyore——"

"If only you were here, then we could think of something to do."

Christopher Robin looked up at Tigger and Roo, and tried to think of something.

"*I* thought," said Piglet, "that if Eeyore stood at the bottom of the tree, and if Pooh stood on Eeyore's back, and if I stood on Pooh's shoulders——"

"And if Eeyore's back snapped suddenly, then we could all laugh. Ha, ha! Amusing in a quiet way," said Eeyore, "but not really helpful."

"Well," said Piglet meekly, "*I* thought——"

"Would it break your back, Eeyore?" asked Pooh, very much surprised.

"That's what would be so interesting, Pooh. Not being quite sure till afterwards."

Pooh said, "Oh!", and they all began to think again.

"I've got an idea!" cried Christopher Robin suddenly.

"Listen to this, Piglet," said Eeyore, "and then you'll know what we're trying to do."

"I'll take off my shirt and we'll each hold a corner," said Christopher Robin, "and then Roo and Tigger can jump into it, and it will be all soft and bouncy, and they won't hurt themselves."

"*Getting Tigger down*," said Eeyore, "and *Not hurting anybody.* Keep those two ideas in your head, Piglet, and you'll be all right."

When Roo understood what he had to do, he was very excited, and cried out, "Tigger, Tigger, we're going to jump! Look at me jumping, Tigger! Like flying, my jumping will be. Can Tiggers do it?" And he squeaked out, "I'm coming, Christopher Robin!" and he jumped—straight into the middle of the shirt.

And he was going so fast that he bounced up again almost as high as he was before, and went on bouncing and saying, "Ooh!" for quite a long time, and then at last he stopped and said, "Ooh, lovely!" And they put him on the ground.

"Come on, Tigger," he called out. "It's easy."

But Tigger was holding on to the branch and saying to himself, "It's all very well for Jumping Animals like Kangas, but it's quite different for Swimming Animals like Tiggers." And he thought of himself floating on his back down a river, or striking out from one island to another, and he felt that that was really the life for a Tigger.

"Come along," called Christopher Robin. "You'll be all right."

"Just wait a moment," said Tigger nervously. "Small piece of bark in my eye." And he moved slowly along his branch.

"Come on, it's easy!" squeaked Roo. And suddenly Tigger found how easy it was.

"Ow!" he shouted, as the tree flew past him.

"Look out!" cried Christopher Robin to the others.

There was a crash, and a tearing noise, and everybody was in a heap on the ground.

Christopher Robin and Pooh and Piglet picked themselves up first, and then they picked Tigger up, and underneath everybody else was Eeyore.

"Oh, Eeyore!" cried Christopher Robin, "are you hurt?" And he felt him rather anxiously, and dusted him and helped him to stand up again.

Eeyore said nothing for a long time. And then he said, "Is Tigger there?"

Tigger was there, feeling Bouncy again already.

"Yes," said Christopher Robin. "Tigger's here."

"Well, just thank him for me," said Eeyore.